TOM RYAN'S SHOES

THE LEGEND OF THE BANSHEE CASTLE

T. A. KEENAN

Published by T.A. Keenan
Middletown, Maryland, USA

This book is a work of fiction. Real historic persons or events may appear in the story; however, the situations and dialogues concerning them are fictionalized. All the events of the story, as told, are products of the author's imagination.

First Paperback Edition

For all the travelers

INTRODUCTION

For a year or more during Covid, I did not step foot in a grocery store. Such was the fear of infection. Fortunately, there was Instacart.

What if there had been no Instacart—nor any supermarkets at all? If all our supermarkets shut down, one by one in the course of a season, how would you survive? Would you forage for nuts and berries in the woods? Try to snare a few rabbits?

Suppose you were able to find, say, a black walnut tree. Assume the nuts were ready to harvest. Would you know how to extract the meat of the nuts from the thick, oily husk? Assume you catch a rabbit—a fat, healthy rabbit. Would you know how to skin, clean, and prepare it? Here on my own rural acres, surrounded by nut trees, with deer and turkey abundant as well, I think one could survive—but only barely, assuming law and order prevailed.

The people of Ireland found themselves in such a state by the Spring of 1845, with the spread of *phytophthora infestans*, also known as potato blight. For 200 years, the potato had been the primary source of food for Ireland's rural poor (the great majority of the population.) Most available grain and livestock was sold to pay rent, collected by middlemen on behalf of the English and Anglo-Irish ruling class. A small garden plot could yield enough potatoes to feed a family. Up to 40% of the population depended almost entirely on the potato for sustenance; for the majority, it was the main source of calories. Repeated potato crop failures in 1845-1849 caused an estimated 1 million deaths and 2 million emigrations, in a population of about 8 million. There was no Instacart.

Now, the ocean surrounding Ireland was teaming with fish. Yet, suitable boats, nets, and other equipment—not to mention knowledge and skills to use them—were all in short supply. Moreover, once fish are brought in from the ocean, they must be processed: dried, canned, or put on ice; transported inland; cleaned; sent to market; and so forth. Ireland lacked the infrastructure to do this at scale for domestic consumption.

As for fish and game in the inland waterways and forests, skills and equipment likewise would have been in short supply. Wealthy landlords controlled the access to fish and game. Poaching laws were strictly enforced. Violation could lead to eviction, tantamount to a death sentence during the famine.

My own Irish great grandparents arrived in America decades after the famine. I wonder how they survived it. Within a few years of settling into a small town in the wealthy state of Connecticut, family and close friends had a man in the legislature; they were running the local fire hall, a charity house, and a filling station. Ours must have been a family already familiar with managing some money and property by the time we arrived. How did relatively fortunate Irish families such as ours acquit themselves during Ireland's time of great need?

Perhaps they never bought into what social scientists have called a "culture of poverty": a system of beliefs and behaviors that can make poor people complicit in perpetuating their own misery. This explanation is controversial. It amounts to victim-blaming; it fails to account for problems in the social, economic, legal, and political frameworks. But to the extent that a culture of poverty exists and plays a role, it surely affects not only the poor, but also those more fortunate. The notion that the poor need only "pull themselves up by their bootstraps," handed down from generation to generation of the well-off, can justify indifference, resignation, and inaction.

Economic and cultural thriving depend on knowledge. The privileged jealously guard it behind veils of arcane language or arbitrary barriers to school admissions. The poor may distrust and belittle the kinds of knowledge the privileged claim, seeing hoaxes and conspiracies at every turn.

Churches and schools were not the only trustees of knowledge and belief. This story features a "woman of knowledge," a bean feasa. She is not to be confused with the "witch" of continental European, British, or American history and legend. Ireland had few witch trials and executions; the bean feasa was typically

respected as a healer, midwife, and advisor—
though in legend she might acquire the power to
shift shapes, control the weather, and so on.

In any event, I am a writer of fiction, not an
historian, not a sociologist, and seldom a church-
goer. One draws on these questions and explana-
tions as elements of a story, one that focuses on a
small cast of characters whose lives, like my own
ancestors' lives, the famine touched but did not
ruin.

So, what would a representative cross-section
of middle-class characters have looked like in late
1840s Ireland? At some level, they must have
had the same virtues and flaws as other authors
have observed in human archetypes since time
immemorial. For a model, I find myself reaching
all the way back to *The Canterbury Tales*. The
Prioress, in this novella, becomes the manager of
a Magdelene Laundry operation. The Miller
becomes, well, a miller. Constance, of The Man
of Law's Tale, is inspiration for the character who
becomes the Hag.

Another inspiration for this story should be
obvious from the name of the pig.

Surely, I have gotten some of the geography,
the language, and the history wrong. If so, one

can only hope the facts do not get in the way of the story. All these characters and plot elements take on a life of their own, of course. May readers enjoy a few hours with the story for its own sake. If it prompts some reflection on deeper questions of social justice, historical or contemporary, all the better.

T.A.K.

Middletown, Maryland, U.S.A.

CONTENTS

PROLOGUE

The line of men spills down the front steps, redolent of perspiration and tobacco smoke.

Amid the chatter, a man named Niall turns to the quiet, nervous fellow behind him and looks him up and down.

"What's your name, bud?"

"Carlo."

It is autumn, 1933. Mid-morning. A rural setting in central Connecticut. On the wall of the white clapboard farmhouse, beside the front door at the head of the line, a brass sign reads:

COLD STREAM FARM

CITY OF MERIDEN

In the farmhouse's main office, visible through the open front door, the line begins in front of a big oak desk. Parked to one side of the building, a large wooden cart is loaded with bushel baskets full of ripe, unblemished red apples. An apple orchard stretches into the background.

A dozen or so men stand ahead of Carlo in the orderly, chattering line. Niall turns again and leans in to make his point.

"Listen, Carlo. Don't you know? Only Irish need apply here."

"Huh?" Carlo looks around sheepishly.

"Just yankin' your chain, bud. I mean, Carlo. Such a place never did exist—not here in America, not back in Ireland neither. Relax.

"A day's wages, three square meals, and a warm bed is what you get here. Any out-of-work Mick, Wop, or Canuck who can do the work! A 'poor farm' is what they call it, but there ain't no shame in it."

A staffer named Quill, hardly four feet tall, strolls down the steps and along the line. He addresses Carlo in a slight Irish accent.

"Clean place. Damn sight better than the workhouses back in the old country."

He casually bites into an apple. Carlo relaxes.

MEANWHILE, Molly, a red-haired woman of about forty, rearranges boxes in the farmhouse attic. She comes upon an old steamer trunk. A faded label reads:

ELIZA RYAN
LIVERPOOL TO BOSTON
MAY 1886

Molly opens the trunk. It is empty, save for a pair of old horsehide shoes. A thick roll of paper is stuffed into the left shoe. Molly pulls it out and unrolls it. She finds several sheets covered in cursive writing in a very fine hand. At the top of the first page is a title:

TOM RYAN'S SHOES

Molly descends the attic stairs to the second-floor hallway, carrying the roll of paper toward an office with a brass sign on the open door, marked:

Deputy Manager

Inside the office, Tommy, a man in his early forties, sits at a large mahogany desk with his back to the door, talking on the phone in a heavy New England accent.

"Yes, Senator... money, we need money. Enough to start up a cider operation. It'll employ a few more workers, but mainly it'll fund some of the other operations..."

Molly waits in the doorway for a moment as Tommy continues talking. Then she walks over and drops the roll of papers on the desk.

Tommy spins around in his office chair to face her as he puts down the phone. His left sleeve is pinned up at the elbow, covering his amputated arm. The left side of his face is badly disfigured.

"Have a look at this, Tommy."

Tommy unrolls the papers and begins reading the first page. He looks up at Molly, then down again as he continues.

"I remember this story. Mom must've written

it down before the cancer took her. Wish I'd taken it to heart before I enlisted."

"You did your duty, Tom."

Quill stands in the doorway, eavesdropping as he eats his apple.

Molly takes a seat as Tom makes another call. As she gazes wistfully out the window, she recalls an evening of storytelling decades before...

A CHILLY EVENING IN 1897, in the same house. A sparrow perches on a slender branch, pecking at an upper-story window.

Inside the large bedroom on the other side of the glass, five-year-old Molly sits on a young woman's lap. Seven-year-old Tommy plays with lead soldiers on the floor. The three are gathered within the circle of a large braided rug. Heat from the fireplace downstairs rises through a floor vent. The woman is thin and sickly-looking. She speaks to the children in a Cork accent.

"Tom and Molly, shall I tell you The Legend of the Banshee Castle? It's about your grandfather."

Tommy looks up, then down again. He makes the sound of cannon fire.

"More Irish malarkey? I'm pretty busy now."

"I see, General Tom. You have a war to manage."

"Oh, but I want to hear!" says Molly.

"Well, all right... but only if you don't leave out the scary parts. Or any bloody bits. Molly can go to bed right now if she's a scaredy-cat."

"I am not a scaredy-cat! I love scary parts and bloody bits too. Tommy's just saying that 'cause he's the scaredy-cat!"

"Yeah, right," says Tom.

"All right, then. Quick, now. Sit up against the bed for support."

Lizzy leans back in the rocker, closes her eyes, and begins reciting the story by heart...

MOLLY AWAKENS FROM HER DAYDREAM. She begins to read the version of the story her mother, Lizzy, transcribed—or wrote, or compiled. The provenance of family stories is seldom clear.

1
———

Mitchelstown

On an October morning in 1846, a full year into the famine, a stiff breeze blows at Tom Ryan's back. A pig trots along at his side as he walks quickly north along the road at the edge of Ballyhooly. A canvas satchel hangs from his right shoulder. A young woman of about eighteen follows closely behind, struggling to keep up.

"Tommy!" the young woman sobs. "I pleaded with him for days. You know that! But this is my home. I can never leave it."

Tom stops short, takes a deep breath, then turns to face her.

"No one expects that now. Go make your father his big Ballyhooly breakfast. Go about your day and forget me. I only wanted you to wait, to give it a chance—not to come with me to Tipperary. You couldn't even promise that. So we were never meant to be. I told you that a week ago."

Tom turns and resumes walking at a determined pace. The young woman remains where she is. A middle-aged woman stands by the road in the middle distance, watching them. Clusters of emaciated vagrants line both sides of the road.

The middle-aged woman steps forward and places a hand on her daughter's shoulder.

"You're a stranger to our ways, Tom Ryan!" shouts the mother. "You'll wind up in the army serving the Queen, just like your cousin Frank. I give it a month. But not with any daughter of mine by your side—or waiting for your return!"

A MILE NORTH, Frank Ryan sits on a stump by the side of the road. A black horse grazes in the lush green grass nearby. From Frank's thumb and forefinger dangles a wriggling worm.

He stares at it intently, as if pondering some deep philosophical question. Then another movement catches his eye. To his left, over the crest of the road toward Ballyhooly, a familiar face appears. Then the shoulders, then the legs. Cousin Tom—and a little critter trotting at his side. A pig.

Frank still holds the worm when Tom catches up.

"For once in your life, you're on time. Learn a thing or two in the army?"

"Aye. The early bird catches the worm."

"Ha! I see that. Breakfast?" Tom asks with a grin.

"I was just asking m'self that. How hungry would a fellow have to get? Well, I'm not there yet."

"Good thing. It's a Friday."

"Aren't you the pious one. I'd be sure to confess it. 'Bless me, Father, for I have sinned—I ate a worm on a Friday!'"

"And I'd say an extra prayer for your immortal soul, Francis. For the worm's, too. But let's not dawdle. It's a good half day over the Galtee Hills—more at the rate you walk."

Frank tosses the worm aside, stands, stretches, and yawns.

They start walking. Frank's riding boots are in good condition. Tom's shoes are badly worn and ill-fitting, with the outline of his toes clearly visible at the tips. Frank nods toward the little pig.

"I wasn't expecting a threesome."

"I thought I'd sell her in town. Should get enough cash for a new pair of shoes. I'll need them before our pilgrimage is done."

"Her? So it's a gilt?" asks Frank as they find their stride.

"She is. A Tamworth, three months old. Thirty pounds now, I'd say. I call her Toto. French slang for derrière, I'm told."

"I never make it a practice to name them."

A loud caw interrupts them. Tom looks to the sky, this way and that, anxiously.

"It's been following me since Ballyhooly. Belongs to the old bean feasa."

"Now don't be starting with her again. Next, you'll be seeing leprechauns darting along the road!"

The raven caws again. A wind whips up. The trees rustle. Tom and Frank bow and turn their heads before a sudden, blinding swirl of dust. The shield their faces in the crooks of their arms. When the little cyclone subsides, there she is, not 20 paces in front of them.

Tom quietly addresses Frank.

"It's the old *Bean Feasa*."

"A foursome it is, Tom Ryan," says she.

Frank clears his throat, still coughing from the dust. "We've no need for company, good woman. Go find shelter. Rest. We have a long walk ahead of us today."

"I'll be the judge—or God Almighty—of when it's my time to rest, buckos. I know this road well. Travel it often. Stay alert and beware. You with your fat little pig, Tom Ryan, and starving people about. You with your fine boots, Frank Ryan, and the White Boys about. I'll stay out of your way, if that's your preference, buckos. But don't you be telling me to rest. I've work to do. Much work. Some of it concerns you, as you shall see soon enough. Good day to you—for now."

The hag cackles as she wanders off onto a side path, hunched over her staff. Tom and Frank look at each other, then at her, then at the road ahead. They continue on their way.

After half a mile, they reach a blighted orchard at the edge of the road to Glanworth. Finnbarr Murphy, about sixty and emaciated, sits facing the road with his back against an apple tree. Two apple cores lie at his side. He holds a small sack in his lap and shreds a slice of stale bread into it, bit by bit. Now and then, he eats a tiny piece.

"Welcome to the Tabard Inn, pilgrims!" he shouts weakly.

"Hello, Finn Murphy!" Tom calls. "Quite a feast you have there. Did you leave any for us?"

"Wormy apples? Many still, and a few more remain atop. Did not have the strength to climb nor to shake the tree."

"But you got your fruit for the day. Meat, too! Have a go at it, Frankie?"

Tom and Frank shake the small apple tree. Several apples fall with a thud. Toto and the horse begin to forage.

Frank lifts a small, blemished apple to his lips.

Tom grabs Frank's arm. "Stop! Better save them for the road."

"Here, put them in your satchel then, Tom."

"No, not with the family Bible."

"Leave it to Frank to bear the bad apples, then. No family Bible in my bag. Always thought it was a Protestant thing, to keep one."

"It's from Mum's side."

Frank stuffs several apples into the satchel at his left side, next to a small whiskey flask. He then turns to Finn.

"You called us pilgrims. You must've spoken to young Jimmy."

"I did, after you dropped off the saddle."

"So, you know what we're about, Finn Murphy."

"I know it. Going against the tide as usual, Frank. April is the month folk long to go on pilgrimages, not October. You're taking the path we came down on, from Nenagh years ago. Me and your fathers. Now you'll take it back the other way?" Finn looks off to the side, into the distance. "Then you're off to America afterwards?"

Frank gives him a wink.

"Aye. If I don't meet a lass on the road to tie me down, first."

"Ha! I'll believe that when I see it. And you, Tommy? Ballyhooly not big enough for your dreams?"

"I'm no dreamer, Finn. It's a practical matter. That railway never seems to come." Tom surveys the landscape as he speaks. "If ever it did, we'd thrive. 'Til then, it's time to spread my wings a bit. Uncle Edmond gave us a standing offer years ago."

"Go up to his place over the mountains, learn a thing or two about running a big operation?"

"A big operation it is. Hundreds of acres," says Tom. "He could use the help for sure. I'll learn more than a thing or two for my efforts. All the art. The know-how. Come back to the land Da left me, make ready to move goods by rail, scale it up, when the rail comes."

Finn smiles at Frank, then looks back to Tom.

"If you don't meet a lass on the road first to tie you down closer, Tom?"

"Not lookin' for that here in Ballyhooly anymore, that's for sure."

"It's not the local girls who won't have us," says Frank. "It's their fathers. Or their angry older brothers. May as well be a Protestant if you've served the Queen."

"Or if your cousin has!" says Tom, glaring at Frank.

There is an awkward pause. Frank looks

down at his own feet. Tom moves away and shuffles around a few small trees, looking up for
apples. In the background, the horse nibbles at
windfalls. Toto roots in the soft earth.

"Whose idea was this journey?" asks Finn in
a low voice, out of Tom's earshot.

"His. He thinks he's master of his fate, now
his father's gone."

"Thought so. You're more a one to go where
the tide takes you."

Frank chuckles.

"I'm not that adrift, Finn. Promised his mum
I'd look after him."

"But he doesn't know about the change?
With Edmond bankrupt and gone?"

"Er ... no. I served under the new owner,
General Bishop. Was about to send him a letter,
then thought better of it."

"Let the boy make his own way?"

"Afraid the general would say 'no.' He'll be
harder to refuse once he's at the general's door.
And another thing: Dinna want Tom to get the
idea we were setting him up."

"Ah. For a stint in the army, you mean?"

"Aye. He's clear that will be his decision. No
one else will sway him. I'll lead the horse to

water is all, then make myself scarce. The big dreams will meet reality in time. 'Til then, I mean to keep his two feet on the straight path, best I can. Out of the faery rings. He's apt to wander. There, see what I mean!"

Tom has started to climb one of the trees. Off to one side, the horse continues nibbling the windfalls.

"A horse has more sense," says Frank. He calls out. "Tommy boy! You're a sprat no more. No need to go climbing, just come down and pick from the windfalls. "

"Not him," says Finn. "He's an eye for the fair apples, that one!"

"C'mon down. The two of us can give the trunk a shake again."

Tom climbed back down and brushed his hands together. Frank walked over. Frank and Tom shook the small apple tree. Several apples fell with a thud. Frank stuffed several more into his deep satchel.

"All but the manky ones are off to England," Finn said quietly. "Barely cover our rents."

Tom now spoke with an air of authority.

"We'll go first to St. B's. The wee shrine. Frank can say a few prayers for his fallen comrades. Then he'll be back down. I'll be over to Bansha and stay for the summer, at least."

"Aye. I'll check back on my mum in Mitchelstown, then here again to see how you're faring. You look thin."

"Not as thin as I look. The heart is stout. Still have a hog to butcher. Thanks for the saddle, by the way."

"Jimmy should get a good price... once you find a buyer."

"A buyer we'll find. But one other thing—watch out for those Roche boys. They've fallen in with some gang."

"Whiteboys or Ribbon Men, likely," Frank said.

"One of 'em. Layin' down the local law, decidin' who's Irish enough."

"Don't I know it," said Frank. "Always reminding us the Roches have been here since Norman times. Never liked us newcomers."

"'Specially not you, Frank. Serving the Queen is another mark against you. Now and again, you've picked up their very accent, even."

"We'll be fine, Finn. They're all talk—helpful, even, if you humour them a bit."

"But people are angry now, Frank," said the

older man. "One violent act makes the next one easier."

"I'd hoped to be done with all that when I mustered out."

"Keep to the straight path, buckos. You'll find what you seek—be it a home, a bride, or a purpose in life."

Tom and Frank paused a minute, said good-bye, and set off with the horse and the pig.

North on the road to Mitchelstown, right at the crossroads to Glanworth Bridge, then north up a rise by the River Funshion, a man in his late fifties sat on the middle limb of a tall tree. Will Robbins had a clear view across the River Funshion toward the Ballyhooly Road—the very road Tom and Frank now travelled.

He nails the last wooden plank of a new observation deck onto the limbs before him.

At the base of the tree, under the edge of the canopy, the old hag leaned on her staff, looking up. A man of about twenty-five, Dick Wilson, stood nearby. He wore black-rimmed pince-nez spectacles attached to a black cord. He looked toward a barn downhill as he spoke to Will in a refined London accent.

"Now that's exactly what we were talking about the other day. A man your age needs to get up and away from the ground vapours. Strong light will strengthen your constitution—once a day at least. Fresh air. Take a little nap, why don't you? Keep you from catching a chill, or worse."

Will responded in a heavy Cockney accent.

"'Tis me observatory. Naught for nappin', mate. Gotta keep me eyes peeled—peeled for them walkin' dead."

"Any of them come this way after the grain, you just call out."

"Right-o. I'll sound the call, you release the 'ounds!"

"They'll keep the thieving Papists at bay, surely. Now, while you're at it, I'll head down to the barn and load the hoppers."

Inside the barn, Dick loaded corn into a hopper. Margaret Robbins entered the mill, smiled at Dick, and glanced back toward her husband in the tree as she closed the mill door and leaned against it. She was a buxom woman in her early twenties.

She watched Dick as he loaded the corn.

"Just what I came to see—a man who knows how to fill my hopper."

"Come over to me then, my little wagon."

Dick dropped a sack of corn on the floor as he gawked at Margaret. Thud!

A few kernels spilled out. Several mice scurried in and began to devour the corn. Soon, the barn came alive with the sounds of Dick and Margaret in the throes of passion.

BACK AT THE TREE, Will heard faint noises coming from the barn. He looked in that direction and started to climb down. He slipped, fell onto the ground, and groaned. In a nearby tree, the raven cawed once.

The hag shuffled up next to Will. She leaned on her staff.

"*Old fool*! What do you expect when you take a young wife you can't trust? That barn is rocking fair near off its stones! And do you really think your treehouse or that pair of old hounds will keep this famine at bay? *Langer!*"

Two harmless-looking old hounds lolled in the sun nearby. Will tried to get up, groaning softly.

"No, no. You just have a little rest and listen to me. I shall help you with your wife and that, that... gombeen man... but first, do you agree to do a small service for me?"

"Anything! Anything to make things right with me Margaret."

"Wait here a little while. Then go into the barn and mill up a sack of that corn from America. Grind it fine, grind it clean. Before an hour passes, take it down to Glanworth Bridge. Give it to the first person you see there."

"Just 'and it o'er free o' charge?"

"Eejit! 'Tis called 'charity,' don't you know it? You shall do this weekly until the famine has taken all its toll. Now, lean your head a little closer here."

The Hag pulled a small blue bottle from within her cloak. She uncorked it and sprinkled a few drops of liquid onto Will's head. His grey hair and beard slowly began to turn black.

"Subtle, now, subtle. Your Margaret will

notice the change soon enough. And remember the tea I left you, last we met."

She lowered her voice nearly to a whisper.

"But tonight, at midnight, go into the barn and turn your millstone once, counter-clockwise. Counter-clockwise, I say. Then go to your Margaret. Repeat this for a fortnight. The results shall please you. And Margaret as well."

The hag cackled.

Tom and Frank approached a crossroads. A sign pointed left, westward, toward Castletown Roche, and straight ahead, northward, toward Mitchelstown. From the north, a peat wagon approached with menacing speed.

A scarf covered the driver's mouth and nose. Tom waved to him politely, but the driver did not return the gesture. He turned west onto the road toward Castletown Roche. After he made the turn, Tom and Frank saw that the back was loaded with emaciated corpses. They both removed their caps in respect.

Suddenly, from one of them, an arm lifted.

Tom gasped and started to run after the wagon. Frank held him back.

"Tom, that's a dead man. The limbs sometimes do that as the stiffness of death sets in."

Tom gulped. A dust cloud followed the wagon as Tom and Frank stood and stared after it.

They resumed their pace. Along the road to Mitchelstown, they came to a side road leading over to Glanworth Bridge.

"Ah, d'you smell that lovely scent?" said Tom. "It's coming up from the river."

"I smell nothing. Too much whiskey and smoke, I've known."

Toto trotted ahead.

"Let's go over. Follow Toto! Maybe pick a few flowers for your mum. Or, with luck, it's that lass on the road Finn mentioned. A fragrant one."

"With her good-looking, fragrant friend, I hope."

They proceeded toward Glanworth Bridge. Frank tied his horse to a post at the west end. As they approached the middle of the bridge heading east, Tom noticed something down in the river to his right. They stopped, rested against the side of the bridge, and looked down. Two corpses floated by—an old man and an old woman.

"Fish food," said Frank.

"I'd hate to be the fish that eat that food."

"I'd hate to be the landlord who eats the fish that ate that food."

Frank turned his back to the river.

"No sympathy for them!" cried Tom. "You or I pull a single trout from this river, next thing we're rotting in some filthy jail for poaching."

"May as well go to the workhouse," said Frank calmly.

As the conversation continued, Frank and Tom watched a man approach from the east end of the bridge. Toto had run ahead to meet him. She turned back, following a small trail of grain spilling from the back of the cart. The stranger had overheard them.

"Aye, you're still be'er off in the filthy work-house than in a filthy jail fer poachin'!"

It was Will Robbins. One arm was in a sling. With his other arm, he led a donkey and cart.

"You'd be the local warden, then?" asked Frank.

"Ha! Nay, I run a mill up a short way. Came down t' bring a sack o' fresh-milled corn, give it t' the first 'ungry passer-by. That's wha' we do, ya know. Chari'y."

"Your arm?" asked Frank.

"This?"

He raised the injured arm slightly.

"Fell out o' a tree. 'Ad to chase the rascal what's been peepin' on me wife! See, 'e tricked me into climbin' that high tree—says the walkin' dead are comin'! 'Get ye to an 'igh place, lest even their vapours waft up an' send ya to the fever 'ouse!' So I climbs the tree, and next thing I spies 'imself by the mill, all up close an' cosy wif me Margaret! Thought you two was 'im and his mate, but now I see you ain't. Well, such are the trials and triboolations of an old man oo takes a young wife. All day, it's one eye mindin' me work and t'other mindin' me Margaret. Canno' trust a soul in this world no more."

"Why marry a woman you couldn't trust?" asked Frank, smiling.

"Well now, one look at me fair young Margaret and you'd know. But now—don't you go gettin' no ideas!"

Tom chuckled.

"Now, now, don't you worry about that! We're headed the other way, besides."

"Where to? Uh, if you don't mind me askin'. Seems all the poor souls are 'eaded up toward Mitchelstown or down to Cork City. To the work 'ouse, the fever 'ouse, or the grave. Look! You can see 'em shufflin' along down there now!"

"We try to avoid them. Me and my cousin Francis here are heading up to St. Berrihert's shrine. Expect the air and water are still clean over that side. You know that area? Glen of Aherlow?"

"Don't know 'bout no Papist shrines and superstitions. No disrespect, but I've enough to mind around me own parts."

Frank leaned in to Tom's ear and said softly,

"His wife's private parts, he means."

Tom grinned.

"Francis here mustered out of the army in September. We'll sell his horse in Mitchelstown, then leave whatever we get for it there with his mum. You need a horse, perhaps? Or a pig?"

"Sorry, lad. One 'orse an' one wife's as much as I can 'andle fer now. No pigs!"

"Well then, we've still a long day's walk, so we'll be going."

"Good day to you, then. Oh—but take a sack of meal. For your good mudder, that is. Send someone up to the mill there, same time weekly, for anudder."

"Thank you."

"Charity—it's what we do. Need to get up to me mill now, before Dick Wilson comes back 'round again to pilfer the Queen's grain—I mean, me grain!"

The large donkey cart interior was empty save for one small sack. Will gave Frank the five-pound sack of Indian meal, gathered by a loop of twine, from the otherwise empty cart. He said goodbye and left after Tom and Frank thanked him again.

Then the two stepped to the north side of the bridge and looked over. Frank pulled out his bottle and took a swig.

"At least the fish are happy amid our misery, swimming about however they please."

"You're not a fish. How do you know the fish are happy?" asked Tom.

"You're not I. How do you know I don't know the fish—or the faeries—are happy? But you asked me the question, so you already knew I knew it! An old Chinaman stepped me through the same conundrum on a bridge in Sevastopol." Frank took another swig. "Back in '42, it was."

"Hm. You know, Frank, I'd never seen a corpse before this morning—other than Nana Murphy at her wake. I suppose you've seen many."

Frank turned away from the river. He put his whiskey flask back in his satchel, then stood erect and brushed himself off.

"Shouldn't we go down and pull those bodies out?" asked Tom. "See they're buried, back there at the Abbey?"

Frank craned his neck back around and down toward the water.

"I take them for suicides. Old man and wife, evicted maybe, couldn't bear to go on."

"Well, they still deserve a decent burial."

"Don't you know, Tommy? No church will bury suicides in consecrated ground. Nature will take its course. I've seen as much, I have—in all its stages. We'd best get moving again."

Frank and Tom returned to the horse. Frank now carried the five-pound sack on his right shoulder. Toto stayed close by Frank, eager for spillage. They set off toward Mitchelstown once more.

As they approached Glanworth Abbey, Tom and Frank saw a woman by the road. She was about thirty-five, prematurely greying and thin. She sat on the ground, bloody hands in her lap, looking down and away from the road. Her two young sons, twins, appeared to be gutting the remains of an animal.

"That's Maude Dyer."

Frank looked straight ahead.

"Don't look at her. She's ashamed. Jimmy told me about her yesterday. Evicted last week."

Around the back of the priory, by the River Funshion, through the open doorway of the Magdalena Laundry building, two long rows of girls stooped over laundry tubs along either window wall. Through the open doorway of an office at the back, the matron stood before a mirror on the window wall, primping. The wavy reflection appeared to show a tall, elegant woman.

She took a seat at a desk in the centre of the

room, facing the doorway. A greyhound sat at her side, gazing up at her adoringly in the direction of the window wall. She picked up a book of French lessons and quietly mouthed a few phrases in French.

A pregnant girl, about sixteen, looking down-cast, entered through the doorway, guided from behind by an older washerwoman whose hands rested firmly on the girl's shoulders. The washer-woman pushed down on the girl's shoulders, then released her.

In Irish, the girl said, "Teastaíonn cúnamh uaim." (I need help.)

"I know you nee—... in English! Ou en français."

The girl stammered.

"I... I..."

The matron sneered.

"You need help. All you brazen hussies need help."

She turned to her dog, mouthing kisses, then fed it a small morsel from a fine china bowl.

"If you'd stayed with your mothers and helped with the baking, you wouldn't come to us with a bun in the oven. Well, at least you did not go to the old woman... for that kind of help. Run along."

To the washerwoman, the matron said,

"Merci pour la présentation."

The washerwoman rolled her eyes. The girl, guided by the washerwoman, turned to leave. The washerwoman reached around to begin closing the office door.

The greyhound looked toward a corner behind the desk, opposite the window wall, where a woman in black was seated, visible at first only from the waist down. She raised a bony hand from her lap and waved it toward the door. The greyhound whimpered, got up, and scurried out behind the washerwoman, who closed the door.

The old hag stood and moved behind the matron. She placed her bony hands on the matron's shoulders and pushed down. She spoke sarcastically.

"How excellent your French sounds, ma chère. And how kindly you treat these poor girls. Stand up. Go to the mirror once more. Let us fix your hair again."

The matron looked up and back at the Hag fearfully. She stood slowly, keeping her head down. The Hag stepped aside and waved her toward the mirror. The mirror clearly reflected the likeness of the stout washerwoman. She raised her hands to her face.

"Fat sow! You show your dog more kindness than you do these girls. I shall help you achieve the respectable air you crave... but first, do you agree to perform a small service for me?"

"Yes—anything!"

"Each week, without fail, provide three packets of clean bed linens to this address."

The Hag handed the matron a slip of paper.

"Bring their dirty laundry back with you. Return it clean and fresh with each visit. Clean and fresh. Now, cock your head to the right."

She did so as the Hag pulled out her blue bottle.

"There, there now—a daub of the finest French lavender. How sweet the smell... and it won't wash off!"

She cackled.

"Now, maybe you'd better go find your dog."

The matron responded in bad French, "Ma chien!"

She rushed out of the office and through the centre of the laundry building. A few young women turned from their washing and scrunched up their noses as they noticed a sickly-sweet smell. The matron ran out through the building door and around to the front of the abbey. There, seven nuns circled round and round, saying their rosaries, eyes downcast, oblivious to all else. The matron cried out the entire way.

"Ma chien! Ma chien!"

She saw her own dog lolling in the grass, wagging its tail and looking happy. But nearby, the creepy twin boys still stood by the other gutted dog, facing the road.

Boy 1: "For soup."

Boy 2: "Pour potage."

Tom and Frank looked at each other, then back toward the front of the Abbey. There, the Hag appeared, bent over her staff and staring at the travellers. Tom and Frank kept walking.

"The old hag again," said Tom.

"Following us?"

Frank chuckled.

"How'd she hobble ahead of us?" asked Tom.

Frank chuckled again, shaking his head.

Tom, Frank, and the pig continue toward

Mitchelstown. The sounds of the horse's footfalls echo behind them.

From atop a hill at Clonlough, above the road approaching Mitchelstown, Mickey Roche and Jack Roche observed Frank and Tom.

"We'll offer them a lift after they leave town and begin to feel the ground rise."

"They'll never get aboard," said Jack. "No love lost between us."

"Oh, they will," replied Mickey. "They'll be tired by then. Remember, they think of themselves as such good Christians—'forgive and forget,' all that malarkey."

"But then..." Jack said. "We need to figure out a way to get them apart. The two of us can manage Frank alone. One by one, we get them out of the way."

"Good idea, Jacky. But it's the boy's name on the deed now. Once he's gone and the tenant leases are up, it's only the mother and old Finn Murphy between us and the land."

They passed a bottle between them, turned, and headed toward a nearby wagon.

In Mitchelstown, at the intersection of Baldwin and Lower Cork Streets, Tom and Frank happened upon a horrifying scene. Dick Wilson stood in a makeshift pillory in the back of a peat wagon. The wagon was stopped just before a crest in the road. A sign labeled him Gombeen Man. One lens of his spectacles was cracked.

A few emaciated vagrants lined the street on either side of the peat wagon. One stood; the others were prostrate or sat on the sidewalks with their backs against the building walls. They observed the scene intently but did not move. The Hag stood bent over her staff to one side of the wagon.

A middle-aged woman ran up to the wagon and cut off a piece of Wilson's right thumb with a single sweep of a sickle. As it fell into the street, Toto trotted toward it. The Raven swept down and beat her to it.

"Justice!" cried a vagrant hoarsely.

A priest in a long black cassock ran out of a house with a crucifix held high. At the sight of the bloody thumb, he doubled over and retched.

"Useless fecker!" cried the Hag. "Go back inside to your drinking!"

"Useless fecker!" cried a second vagrant.

"Useless fecker!" croaked a third vagrant, barely audible.

Another old woman in the crowd crossed herself. Tom and Frank looked on.

"Frank! The Hag again—arrived ahead of us from the abbey."

"Hm. She must have wings under that cloak."

A tall man with an erect bearing approached from around a corner behind them. He took up a position beside Tom, watching the scene. The vagrants, almost in unison, turned their heads toward the bailiff.

"The same wagon will be back for these vagrants," said the bailiff to Tom. "Dead or alive, by tomorrow morning."

Frank leaned forward, past Tom, to address the bailiff on his left.

"And who might you be, sir?"

"Robinson. Bailiff for Viscount Doneraile, High Sheriff of County Cork."

"Was it you who sent the wagon?" asked Frank.

"Aye. We're culling the bad apples, like Wilson there. Been pilfering grain and reselling it for months. Havin' his way with the tenants' daughters, even."

"Must keep you busy. Irishmen have many daughters."

"Aye…"

The bailiff laughed.

"…but most of my work is hauling away these vagrants. The shopkeepers, the residents—no one wants to see them."

"Enjoy your work, do you?"

He turned to Frank and glared.

"I consider myself a Christian man. I do my duty. But if you must know, I need a change of scene."

"Where are you bound?" asked Frank.

"A Major Mahon offered me better terms. Says conditions are not so bad there. Up in Roscommon."

"Good luck to you, sir," said Tom. "We'll be on our way now."

Tom and Frank led the horse into a lane off the main road north. They passed a tailor's shop. On display in the window was a man's long coat. A sign in the window advertised it:

BEWARE OF ASSASSINS!
PROTECTIVE GARMENT FOR SALE
SHOT-PROOF, BALL-PROOF

Inside, visible through the window, a well-dressed man eyes the garment and talks to the tailor as the two gesture toward the garment.

Tom and Frank approached a nearby stable. Frank led the horse inside as Tom waited outside. Toto followed Frank in. Out of curiosity, Tom started heading east down the lane toward the sound of singing and dancing. Behind him, Frank came back out without the horse. Toto came out too, her snout covered in horse shit. Frank put a small bundle of two-pound notes into his satchel, looked about for Tom, then spotted him down the street.

"Hey, Tom!" he cried.

Tom Ryan turned back to join Frank outside the stable.

"We'd best avoid saloons."

"Well, aren't you the abstinent one, suddenly."

"No, it's the fever going around that scares me. It finds its way among crowds."

The two went back the way they came.

At the same moment, in an apothecary shop on Lower Cork Street, a tall, thin, bespectacled chemist waited on a well-dressed customer.

"Oh yes, milady. You can rely on this. Always. For prevention or relief of fever—everything. As bleach is to cleanliness, this is to health. Keeps the humours in balance. Take a spoonful with tea every morning."

She paid the chemist, took a bottle, and left. The chemist locked the door behind her, drew the shade, then went behind the counter. With shaking hands, he pulled out a bottle of laudanum and gave himself a few drops. As he took it, he glanced toward a corner behind the counter, where an old woman in black was seated.

"How excellent your knowledge, dear doctor," said the hag sarcastically. "And how thoughtfully you treat your clients' needs."

She reached into her cloak for her blue bottle.

"Shall we add a few drops of my own special preparation to your daily dose?"

He took a step back, nervously.

"Daily dose? I take but a little, for a headache."

"Lying quacksalver! You take their money and waste it away on your own addictions. You know nothing about healing—not the old ways nor the new. I can offer nothing to the likes of you but a threat, and mark my words, I shall make good on it if you do not perform the service I request. You see this plant?"

She drew a flowering plant from a satchel at her feet.

"It blooms along the banks of the River Funshion this time of year. At dawn each day, gather one plant about to bloom—only one. Grind it fine, grind it clean. Make a decoction. Deliver it by noon each day to this nearby address."

She handed him a slip of paper.

"If you fail in this, you shall be cursed like Tantalus with an unslakable thirst for all the rest of your days. Understood?"

"Yes, yes—you can count on me!"

"I knew I could."

The Hag left the shop and disappeared into the streetscape. Overhead, the raven cawed twice.

Tom and Frank arrived back at the intersection they had left earlier. All the same vagrants were there, plus a few more. With the peat wagon and the bailiff gone, Tom and Frank suddenly found themselves the new centre of attention. Heads turned; an old woman pointed in their direction. Two boys rushed toward them, begging. Soon they were surrounded by the strongest of the emaciated vagrants.

One boy grabbed at Tom's satchel. Tom, Frank, and the small crowd of beggars swirled in confusion until a constable rushed in to break it up. Tom and Frank stumbled out of the swirl and proceeded, shaken, onto the west side of Baldwin Street.

"You all right, Tommy?"

"Yes. I think so. I was scared, Frank."

He gulped.

"I, too."

The two walked at a quick pace, looking straight ahead with sombre expressions. Toto followed behind, distracted by morsels of rubbish and horse droppings.

They reached a wee house on Baldwin Street near Kingston College.

Tom and Frank approached the door, which bore a sign marked "Quarantine." Frank knocked. There was no response. He knocked a second time.

"George? Nellie? Are ya in there?"

A young woman replied in a feeble voice.

"Frankie? Is that you? You know we cannot let you in."

"Nellie, darling, open the window a crack and we'll talk through it."

Frank glanced one way, then the other, up and down the street.

Nellie, about eighteen, went to a window to the right of the door and opened it a few inches.

Frank stooped slightly toward the window.

"Where's Georgie now?"

"He's on the wee bed behind me, sleeping. We have the fever, Frank."

"And Mum? Where's Mum?"

"In rag order, Frank. Typhus. She can barely get up from her bed. They've closed off her doorway with blocks o' sod, save for a wee hole. We pass her water and porridge."

"Ah, Nellie, I did not expect this."

Frank turned around and leaned his back against the wall in despair, his eyes shut.

"But Frank, it's not so bad. We're on the mend, I know it. The old woman comes by."

"The old woman? What old woman?"

"Why, the old widow. The Bean Feasa. Some call her the Hag, but she has a name, you know. Mrs. King. She's getting us food, healing herbs, fresh laundry even. So you needn't change your plans or even worry on our account."

She paused to stifle a cough.

"Just go—the sooner the better. Then send for us after you're settled. 'Tis what we want."

Frank turned back to face the window.

"Look, I'll be back to check on you after I see Tommy up to the Glen. Meantime, take this."

He handed Nellie the bag of Indian corn and a small wad of two-pound notes.

2

The Galtee Mountains

By late afternoon, Tom and Frank grew weary from hunger and exertion. They came to the edge of a great demesne, with a grand manor visible in the distance. A wagonload of vagrants passed them, followed by a constable on horseback. They stopped near a large, makeshift shed attached to an old smithy. Several of the vagrants were recognisable from the streets of Mitchelstown. The constable hustled the vagrants out of the wagon and toward the opening of the shed.

A sign by the shed entrance read:

Famine Relief

First Salvation, then Soup

"You're not goin' in there, are you, Frankie? You can smell it as well as I—it's beef they're serving on a Friday."

"I'll go in with eyes open. I know it—they're soul-jobbers. But I'm fair starving. And I've done worse in the army than eat meat on a Friday."

Frank entered the shed, leaving Tom outside. Toto followed. Inside, he saw a small crowd of men, women, and children seated before a neatly dressed preacher who wore a large gold cross around his neck. A five-person choir sang hymns.

The preacher motioned for the choir to stop, then raised both hands, signalling the crowd to rise. He spoke with an English accent.

"And now, all stand. Let us swear allegiance to the Queen and renounce the Roman Catholic Church, forswearing all Popish belief. Arise!"

All stood.

"Now form an orderly line, that your bodies be nourished, now that your souls are cleansed."

The congregation formed a line. Some elbowed their way ahead.

"Orderly, now!"

An old man at the front knelt and made the sign of the cross before the low serving table, as if to receive communion.

"None of that popery! Rise up, old man, and be born again!"

Toto pissed all around the oblivious preacher's shoes.

After Frank finished eating, he exited the shed and handed Tom a piece of bread. Tom glared at him as he took the bread and tossed it to the ground.

They followed a path along a brook as the mountain shadows grew long. At a bend in the path, they came upon a horrifying apparition. A mother and three children—one of them a babe in arms—shuffled toward them. They were barefoot, filthy, and dressed in tattered rags. Their bones protruded. Their jaws hung slack.

As they met Tom and Frank, the woman

stopped, said nothing, and extended the swad-
dled infant in her shaking arms toward Frank.
Speechless and confused, Frank took the infant.
Immediately, he saw the child was dead. The
woman shuffled past with her other two children,
who looked barely alive. They exchanged no
words.

Frank set the pitiful little corpse on the
ground a few feet to the side of the path. He
made a hollow in the earth with a stout stick,
placed the infant inside, and built a cairn around
it. Tom stood frozen and speechless for several
minutes before he helped gather stones.

Shortly after they set the last stone and
returned to the path, a wagon approached,
carrying vagrants from the shed. A constable
followed on horseback. Tom and Frank stepped
aside to let them pass. They followed along for
half a mile or so, until the constable hustled the
vagrants out of the wagon and toward a hovel at a
crossing.

"Out of the wagon!" barked the constable.

A young couple lingered in the wagon.

"Out, I say!"

The man climbed down, then helped his
pregnant wife. The moment her feet hit the

ground, the wagon lurched forward. She lost her balance and nearly fell.

The constable looked away from the couple toward the others.

"Now stay out of Mitchelstown, all of you. I mean it!"

The constable and the wagon departed. The pitiful passengers sought shelter in the hovel.

"See these footprints?" said Frank. "Three sets. The starving wraiths we passed. This was their home. Must've run out of food, then out of peat."

"The wagon did not pick them up. Where do you suppose they went?"

"Either they found the soup kitchen, or wandered off into the woods to die."

"Shouldn't we go back to look?"

"Tommy... there are too many of them for us to save. Keep a distance. We'll be lucky not to catch a fever from handling the poor babe."

Tom and Frank continued on their way.

Perhaps a half hour's walk later, Tom and Frank came upon another bend in the path beside a merry brook, shrouded in fog. In that place stood a large tent housing another soup kitchen. There were only three men, each very small in stature. They offered a fine fish stew.

One of the wee men stood at the entrance, motioning Tom inside.

"Come in, young man. Come in! Sit yourself down—you look weary."

Tom hesitated and looked to Frank.

"Go ahead, Tom. They're Quakers. They won't steal your soul. I'll wait here. My belly aches."

Tom entered and took a seat. He was the only person in the tent besides the three servers. One of them, whom the others called Paddy, stirred a large pot of soup. The pot steamed, though there was no sign of a fire.

Another wee man ladled soup into a large bowl and set it before Tom. The third set out a tin bowl of soup for Toto. He then took a seat at the head of the table beside Tom. Striking a match against the sole of his shoe, he lit a clay pipe. He looked at Tom intently as he smoked.

"Where do you come from—today, I mean?"

"Ballyhooly."

"Oh, Ballyhooly. Bally*hooooly*." He blows a smoke ring. "And where might ye be goin'?"

"My Uncle Edmond's place, up over the hills, at the east end of the Glen."

"Well now, that's a wee bit o' walking— twenty-five miles, maybe, all told? Not so far. But if it's all wearin' those shoes I saw you come in on, your feet must be hurtin' already."

Tom smiled, nodded, and sighed wearily.

"They do."

"I do a fair bit o' walkin' meself, in this profession I find meself in lately. Last month we ran a kitchen up there in Roscommon—a place called Stroke-stown. Walked the whole way from Dublin, twenty-five miles a day. No, wait... took us six days, didn't it, Paddy?" he said to the one who had ladled the soup.

"Six days, it did. Over a hundred miles total."

"But I always see to it I'm well shod before I set out travelin'."

The wee man's shoes appeared fine-fitting and beautifully made.

"But you know, 'tis a good thing for the feet to suffer a bit now and again. How far do you suppose our Lord walked to Calvary—and that with a mighty cross on his back?"

"I... I wouldn't know, sir."

"Nor would I. A hard thing to reckon, the sufferin'. But now and again, 'tis good for the soul to consider it."

"My uncle—and my father too, for a time— they were soldiers. My cousin Frank as well, outside there. I suppose they each endured many a long march."

"Indeed," said the wee man sadly.

AFTER FINISHING HIS SOUP, Tom left to rejoin Frank, who sat on a rock staring up at the stars. Soon the two lay down for the night on beds of straw and leaves a little way from the brook.

Tom dreamed. He saw the right hand of a young woman passing over plants by the brook. They burst into bloom.

Tom awoke to see the wee man seated on a nearby rock, smoking his clay pipe beside a gently crackling fire. Frank snored.

"Oh, 'tis you, my friend."

Tom sat up and sniffed.

"Do you smell... oh!... 'tis the scent of Easter lilies, in October. Do you smell them?"

The glow of the fire illuminated the wee man's face.

"I do. And if you can, 'tis a good sign—a sign you are soon to marry, perhaps. Meanwhile, are you ready to hear a tale? Well, ready or not, I shall tell you one about Lady Edith of Mitchelstown Castle."

The storyteller's face, illuminated by the fire, appeared to float in the black night sky.

"For her eighteenth birthday, a family friend painted Lady Edith's portrait. The painter sent it out to a shop for framing. By and by, a rich young man spied the portrait in a shop window, set in a circular gold frame. He fell instantly in love with the beautiful young woman in the picture.

"He arranged to meet Lady Edith. Soon he proposed, and she agreed.

"However, he revealed that he was Catholic. Lady Edith's family insisted he convert to the Church of Ireland. He agreed, and a grand wedding was held.

"But the man's own family could not tolerate his marrying a Protestant. On the morning after the wedding, they quarrelled with him. He fell down a flight of stairs, struck his head, and died.

"Claiming she was an enchantress, his family had the young widow abducted.

"They put a hood over her head, bound her hands, seated her in a currach, and pushed it into the River Blackwater, where it flows to the Celtic Sea—placing her fate, they said, in the hands of the Almighty.

"For a time, the vessel drifted toward the sea, but then spun round and round in a dizzying motion that carried it aground. Lady Edith staggered ashore, wandered into a faery ring, lay down, and fell asleep."

"On Midsummer Eve, when the faeries found her and removed her hood, they were enchanted.

"She dwelt among them for a fortnight but would not take their food. She lived on sorrel and such, picked with her own hands.

"'Twas then that she learned the ways of the Other Folk, and also how it feels to be hungry and cold.

"The Good People fashioned a litter for the currach, using poles of ash and cross-braces of yew. Aloft, they carried Lady Edith, weak with hunger, north along the east bank of the Blackwater, turning west at Cappoquin, then north again at Fermoy. Always they kept the river to their left. Their long path was ever on land, for the Good People cannot cross a body of water."

The wee storyteller's face loomed large, illuminated by the fire. It appeared to float in the black night sky above Tom's crude bed. The story continued.

"Thus, Lady Edith made her way back to Mitchelstown Castle—down to the sea and back again in a great gyre—with the Good People's help. Early in the next year, she bore a child... but no other man would have them, despite her wealth and beauty. For a price must be paid when a pregnant woman steps into a fairy ring, whether deliberately or not."

By now, Tom was once again sound asleep. Toto rooted for acorns. At dawn, he and Frank awoke to find the little men—and every sign of them—gone. But by Tom's side were new shoes, with a note tucked inside the left one, written in a very fine hand: "Farewell! May you never wear a soldier's buttons."

As they set out the next morning, Tom's new shoes squeak. He quietly ponders his dreams. He and Frank soon find themselves on the south-facing slope at the west end of the Galtee Mountains. Along the path, a great peat wagon creaks up, drawn by a haggard old nag with blood-red eyes. Driving it are a pair of local bullies, familiar to Frank and Tom: Mickey Roche and his brother Jack, all dressed in white. Mickey offers to take Tom and Frank up to the Glen of Aherlow in the wagon. Frank shrugs. He and Tom are tired already. They climb into the back with Toto.

A LITTLE LATER, before reaching the crest of the mountains, Frank and Tom see two men—one about twenty-five and the other about fifty— nattily dressed in hunting attire. They stand several hundred yards from the wagon path. As the wagon pulls away, a stag grazes uphill from the hunters. One of the men shoots and kills the stag. Immediately, two immense hounds set upon it and begin to tear at its flesh.

Jones

"My dear Mason," says the younger man calmly, in an upper-class English accent. "Your hounds are out of control... Gad! What a waste of fine meat!"

"See here, Jones. We are only out for sport

today. Besides, the family does not much care for venison."

"Yes, but people are starving nearby."

"Potato eaters. Venison would only sicken them. Their constitutions are delicate. And surely you realize that, without a few men along, we are not about to carry out our own kill. English gentlemen are not beasts of burden. Besides, the hounds are hungry, too. It cannot be helped that they are unruly Irish hounds. But I do concede... my man should have done a better job training them."

On a rock cropping a little way uphill from the hunters, the Hag leans on a staff and observes them below. A raven caws. The two hunters look up.

"Look over there now, sir. Who is that? Oh my—another kind of sport, I'd say."

"One more to your liking, eh, Jones?"

They see a lovely young woman, a leannán sídhe, where the Hag had stood. As they approach just below her, Jones is leering. She stands motionless. Mason reaches up as if to grab at her ankles. He looks up and observes, in horror, that she is the Hag.

"Vile rakehell!"

SHE STRIKES her staff twice on the rocks.

Two feral pigs run from the scene, down the hill. The two immense hounds give chase. The squealing swine flee into a small hole among the rocks.

THE WAGON HAS NOW PASSED over the crest to the north side of the Galtees, on the path to Moor Abbey. A cottage doorway, uphill from the road, presents a clear view of the path below. The cottage is little more than a rounded mound of earth covered in vines, but with a large, well-crafted window in the center. A stone chimney at one end emits a wisp of blue smoke. A shadowy figure by a woodpile, stooped and cloaked, carries a blue bottle in her left hand.

The Hag's bony hand brushes over some thorny weeds. After she passes, the weeds wilt at her touch. The same right hand, now youthful, brushes across some tall plants. After she passes, the plants suddenly bloom. She approaches a heap of rocks surrounding a small pool of water.

She stoops to fill the blue bottle. She stands and shakes it gently, never losing sight of the wagon below.

The raven sits on the cottage roof, spreading its wings wide. Its beak opens as if to caw.

"Jack, stop a moment, will you?"

"Whatever for?" asks Jack.

"I need to go shake the dew off my lily."

Jack pulls in the reins. The wagon stops. Tom jumps out. He walks up to a nearby tree to relieve himself, all the while looking about. Out of curiosity, Tom starts to head up a narrow path toward the cottage, but Frank calls him back. Tom returns to the wagon, which creaks away into a mist.

Meanwhile, the Hag shuffles downhill, takes a few pinches of dirt from the base of the tree where Tom relieved himself, and puts them into the blue bottle. She shuffles back up to her cottage.

A soldier soon approaches the cottage on foot from downhill. He crosses the road where the wagon had stopped and proceeds toward the cottage. He stops at the door and removes his cap respectfully. He knocks. The Hag invites him in. He enters.

The soldier finds the Hag seated in a rocker by a gentle, crackling fire. She looks him up and down.

"I know what you've come for, young man. Come warm yourself by the fire."

The soldier takes a seat on a stool by the fire.

"You were told I can tell the future, eh? We'll come to that. But first, what have you brought me?"

The soldier hands her a flask of poteen. She uncorks it and smells.

"Very well, then. If I tell you what you want to know, do you agree to perform a small service for me?"

He nods.

"I shall tell you, then. Your loved ones shall survive this terrible famine. We have ways to provide fresh meat for the local folk. Few will starve here in the Glen. So you may go away to fight your wars, free from worry on that account.

And you shall survive your soldiering. Beyond that, all I can say is that the wars shall change you, and the famine shall change this land. Upon your return, Ireland will not look the same to you. But in time..."

She looks wistfully out the window.

"...after my time, and yours too, perhaps..."

She raises her right hand up and down, as if striking her staff on the floor.

"...Ireland shall be peaceful, prosperous, and free!"

She looks out the window, then back at him.

"Now, about that service... First, take this poultice."

She shakes some dirt from the blue bottle onto a leaf in her lap, molds it into a ball, and hands the leaf-wrapped mud to the soldier, who hesitates.

"Go ahead—it won't hurt you. Put it into your pocket. Now go have a rest on the wee bed there.

"Do not move from the bed until you hear the raven caw thrice. Then go down by the river. There you will find a great peat wagon and horse. Rub the poultice on the horse's nose. Gently. Then get into the wagon. The horse will take you

where you need to go. You will find three widows
by a great iron gate. Their husbands fell in the
Afghan wars; they demand to know where their
men are buried. You shall know what to do for
them. In the back of the wagon, you shall find a
pair of boots. Give them to a young man you find
by the gate. You shall know what to tell him. Can
you remember all that, or do I need to make a
list?"

She cackles.

THE FOUR TRAVELERS arrive in the wagon at
Moor Abbey, on the north side of the Galtee
Mountains.

"Here's as far as we go, boys," declares
Mickey. "Our fishing spot is nigh."

They all get out to stretch.

A wooden stairway reaches up to a door in
the old entry portal below the main stone tower.
The door and stairway appear to be built of
freshly cut timber. A pair of U-brackets flank the
door on either side. A beam, sized to secure the
door from the outside, hangs by a cord on one of
the jambs.

"Looks like the old place is being put to new use," observes Frank. "You've been up here before? Lately, I mean."

"We go here, we go there," says Mickey. "Now and again, we lodge in the tower on our way over to Clonmel. Not the finest hotel, but it'll do in a pinch."

Meanwhile, Tom leans against the wagon and removes a shoe as Toto wanders into the woods. He gives it a shake, as if to dislodge a pebble. As he does so, his shoeless foot comes down on a nettle.

"Ow!" he cries loudly. "I've stepped on a nettle!"

Tom limps about in a tight circle, then goes back to lean on the wagon.

"I don't think I can walk."

Mickey looks at Jack and smiles.

"Tommy boy," says Mickey, "you'd better rest here while we fish."

"Might be wise," says Frank.

Mickey takes command.

"Jack, why don't you and Frank turn the coach around? I'll help our guest up to his quarters."

As Frank climbs up into the front of the

wagon, Jack walks around to the other side. Mickey leans close to Jack as he passes and mutters softly:

"Distract Frank while I tend to the boy."

Tom begins to hobble away toward the tower. Mickey rushes over to support him. The two walk up the stairs and into the tower. Meanwhile, Jack and Frank turn the wagon around.

Mickey reemerges from the tower door. He sees Jack pointing down and away from the tower. Frank, with his back now turned, looks off in that direction. Mickey takes the opportunity to bar the tower door from the outside. He hops into the back of the wagon.

Off they clatter. Tom leans out the lower tower window, smiling, and shouts after them:

"Bring back the Salmon of Knowledge, Frankie!"

Jack turns toward the tower and smiles.

"Now there's a true son of the sod. Knows his Irish lore, Frankie."

"Respect the gods and spirits, but keep your distance from them," mutters Frank, apropos of nothing much.

"How's that?" asks Jack.

"Something an old Chinaman once taught
me, when I was off in the wars."

"You're back in Ireland now, Frank Ryan,"
responds Jack indignantly.

Inside the tower, in his room at the top, Tom
notices a pair of broken, black-rimmed pince-nez
spectacles on the floor. Nearby, the floor is spat-
tered with what appears to be dried blood. Tom
hobbles down the stairway. He discovers the door
is barred from the outside. He hobbles back up.

After a while, Tom hears the sound of
someone singing sweetly nearby.

He goes to the tower window to look out.
Down below, he sees a slender young woman
gathering sorrel and flowers into a hand basket.
She tosses acorns to Toto. Tom shouts down
to her.

"Hello! Hello, young lady!"

She looks around, stands erect, then looks
straight up at Tom.

"What would you be wanting from me,
shouting out like that?"

"Your hand in marriage, perhaps?"

"Oh... would that be all, now?" she replies
sarcastically.

"Your singing—'tis so lovely. I smelled your flowers, too. So sweet!"

"Smelled my flowers all the way up there, did you? Load of malarkey. Did you not smell the raspberry tart I ate for breakfast, too?"

"No disrespect intended. How is it your father allows you to wander about so freely? These are rough times we're in."

"I have no father, only a guardian. She is well respected in these parts. Feared, even. Besides, I have my own wits about me. Learned from the best teacher—the healing arts... and more."

"Clearly. But if you need time to think on my proposal, perhaps you'd first unbar the door below for me?"

"So, it's two things you want from me now. Then, in fairness, I'll be asking two things from you. First, tie your shoes together and throw them down to me. I'll unbar the door, but in the time it takes you to shoe up, I'll be off."

"Ah, fair enough—and clever, too. Look, you needn't worry about my intentions. I can hardly walk, let alone chase after you. I stepped on a nettle."

"A nettle?"

She looks around at the ground.

"Why, there's an herb for that. Let's see, is it that one? No, no. The leaves look right, but it should be about to bloom by now... Oh, there!"

She picks a weedy-looking green plant, then holds it up toward Tom.

"See this?"

"Lovely."

"Lovely is as lovely does. When you toss me your shoes, I'll place a piece inside. Which foot is it?"

"The right one."

"Fine. Now, before you shoe up, don't put a sock on that foot. Let this plant press against the wound. Then proceed to walk around this lawn three times, counterclockwise. No, wait—that's for a different problem. Make it clockwise. Clockwise. Can you remember that, or do I need to leave a list?"

"Your instructions are clear. Now, what was that second request you were about to give me?"

"Oh, yes. In case you'd have a mind to—and I don't mean to presume—but if you do have a mind to come calling on me properly, even in these rough times, as you call them, you'd better be prepared to answer me one question."

"What would that be, Madame Constable? I

suppose you'd first like to know why I came to be locked up here?"

"That? You're so sure you know who barred the door in the first place? Perhaps it was I, perhaps another. Hardly a week goes by that those White Boys don't toss some hapless land-lord or agent into this tower. Not that you sound like a landlord."

She pauses a moment.

"What you'll tell me is this: What do you think it is that women want? If I like your answer, well then, perhaps we shall spend more time together... or perhaps not."

"I see."

Tom ties his shoes together and tosses them down. The young woman unbars the door. By the time Tom hobbles down and puts on his shoes—leaving off the right sock—she is gone.

As he begins to walk in circles, the Hag appears in a black cloak, bent over her long staff. Her long gray hair hides much of her face. She cackles at Tom.

"I heard it all, heard it all!"

She cackles again.

"I know the girl and know her mind well. So

would you like to know the answer your young beauty expects?"

"Why, yes."

"Don't stop now. Keep walking, Tom Ryan! You've only gone halfway around once!"

Tom continues hobbling around the circle as the Hag speaks.

"Now, if I tell it to you and she likes it, I'll be wanting something in return!"

"Anything. Well... within reason."

"Ha! You're the first I've heard put conditions to me. We shall get to what I want when the time comes. For now, let me tell you this, young man. What a woman wants..."

She pauses, looking Tom up and down.

"...is sovereignty over her man. To be mistress of the house and all his affairs. And most of all, for you, with your greater brute strength, to yield this to her willingly, without coercion. Not from her father, not from the Church, and not from the Royal Irish Constabulary!"

She cackles loudly.

Tom looks down. He pauses in thought. By the time he looks up again, the Hag is gone.

In the middle of all this, Tom has completely

forgotten his hunger and his cousin Frank as well. He sits down, takes off his right shoe, feels the wound, and smiles. After putting the sock and shoe back on, he takes a few steps gingerly, then looks toward an opening in the path the young woman had taken. Toto waits for him there.

The Roche boys take Frank down to the River Aherlow in the wagon.

"What is this big iron pot for?" he asks.

"That pot?" says Jack. "Why, it's for the fish, of course."

"And your nets? Where are your nets?"

"Oh, we don't want to tip off the warden if we're stopped," replies Jack. "We leave them in a secret place by the spot."

Mickey stifling a laugh.

"Right," he snickers. "A secret place."

Frank continues to question them.

"Isn't it chilly for fishing? Late in the year and late in the day?"

"Teach you all about fishing in the army, did they, Frankie?" responds Mickey. "The Queen's army?"

"Never been fishing in all my life. Seems the landlords own every fish in every river in Ireland, as you well know."

"Such a dryshite, Frankie!" says Jack. "Don't worry about it. We know a safe spot. On a sunny afternoon, with winter approaching, they'll be biting for sure. Leave it to us."

"That's right. We'll take care of you too, Francis," says Mickey.

When they reach the river's edge atop a high bank, Mickey suggests Frank remove his boots so as not to frighten the fish.

"Those hobnails on the stone—they clatter. The rock is smooth; it won't hurt your feet."

When Frank steps barefoot toward the river's edge, Mickey creeps up from behind and tosses a loop of rope over Frank's head and around his arms. The other end is tied to the great iron pot. Mickey and Jack heave the pot into the river. The pot drags Frank below the surface. Bubbles break above a small sucking vortex, where several dragonflies flit about.

"And such is the end of poor Frank Ryan," declares Mickey. "Frank Ryan, who served the Queen and took the soup!"

A short way up the hill behind them, someone observes the entire scene. A crow caws.

Mickey and Jack look up.

The Hag stands above them on the hill, leaning into her staff. They begin to approach her.

"Are you lost, old woman? Eyesight not so good?"

"My eyesight is excellent," she says sternly. "You have no idea."

Mickey addresses her in a mockingly cordial tone.

"Still, let us bring you down here and help you along your way."

"Merciless manslayers!" she cries.

The Hag strikes her staff twice on a rock. Below her, two little donkeys begin to bray. The raven caws three times and takes flight to the east.

Within the hour, the soldier leaves the Hag's cottage and clambers down the hill to find the wagon. Following her instructions, he rubs the poultice gently around the horse's nose as he caresses her head and murmurs to her. Then he climbs up into the wagon, takes the reins, and heads off to the east.

Meanwhile, on a wooded path leading downhill from Moor's Abbey, Tom sets off to the northeast with the pig. Here and there, he stops to pick up a flower the fair-haired girl had dropped along the way; sometimes the pig beats him to it. Then he disappears into a mist that envelops the wooded path as a great cloud bank moves over the Galtee Mountains.

Tom descends the mist-shrouded path from Moor Abbey into the open glen. He comes to a crossing. Disoriented, he starts to turn left, but a sign by the path reads:

NOT THIS WAY, YOU FOOL!

He turns around and heads east with the pig.

Within the hour, Tom reaches the edge of the O'Ryan demesne on the outskirts of Bansha. He gasps as he approaches the front gate. Three young women, all dressed in black, hang there by their necks. The woman in the center wears a crucifix. The woman on the right wears a plain cross. The woman on the left wears neither, but her cloak is fastened with a clasp in the shape of a Celtic knot.

As Tom draws closer, the peat wagon creaks up to the gate and stops. The soldier looks at the three women intently, then at Tom, who approaches with Toto from across the street.

"Good day to you, soldier. My name is Ryan. Are you here for these women?"

"Yes. Their husbands were killed in the Afghan wars. They asked General Bishop, the new lord of this manor, for their bodies."

"New lord? This is my uncle Edmond's home."

"No more. The former owner went bankrupt. The Crown took the home and gave it over to the General for his services. He is setting operations right again, I hear. But he could not accommodate these poor widows, I hear. They hanged themselves in protest—or despair, I believe. I shall see to their burial. Looks like we have a Catholic, a Protestant, and... I do not know, maybe a pagan."

With an air of authority, Tom declares, "They are suicides, then. No church will bury them in consecrated ground."

With dawning recognition, his tone softens.

"I recognize one of them from the Glanworth way. She worked in the laundries, I think, till she ran off with her soldier."

The soldier pauses in thought for a few seconds.

"I'll have them taken down to Glanworth Abbey and buried by night, in the ground over the caverns."

"I know the place well. Next time I'm there, I shall stop to pray for their souls. By the way, I recognize this horse and wagon."

"A pair of boots is in the back. Do you recognize them as well?"

Looking into the wagon, Tom sees the wet, muddy boots and gulps.

"My cousin Frank's."

"I am sorry to tell you he drowned. Must have slipped and hit his head whilst fishing in the River Aherlow."

Tom's face grows ashen. He grasps the wagon to steady himself.

"Frank was a good swimmer."

The soldier pauses before speaking.

"Sometimes the nets tangle a man up and drag him down."

"Were there no others with him? Two men?"

"Yes, I had seen him with a pair of men. Perhaps they fell in as well, or were taken away for poaching."

Tom touches the boots, then draws back.

"Frank's... my cousin's... my cousin's body?"

"Washed away. An old bean feasa saw it all. Said he was dead for sure and the body would never be found. I know her. She has the sight."

"A so-called witch?"

"You know we do not use that word. Nor do we hang nor burn them. 'Women of knowledge,' we call them. She summoned a priest. He sprinkled holy water on the site and said a few prayers. No different from her methods, to my mind. I came upon them as I walked along the river. She bade me take his boots and ask around here after him. By the look of his boots, he was a soldier too?"

Tom sees the soldier's boots are identical to Frank's.

"He was a soldier. You've done right by a

fellow soldier. If indeed he's gone. With no body, I mean…"

"I regret to bear such terrible news. I don't mean to be cruel. But if your cousin was a soldier, then he accepted—"

He catches himself, pauses a moment, then looks up at the unfortunate women.

"Now, would you help me take these poor souls down? Then I'll be on my way with them."

Tom nods.

"By Monday I'll be back at Victoria Barracks, should you need me. The name is Sheehan. Lieutenant."

As Tom and the soldier take down the bodies, General Bishop and Mr. Quinn walk from the manor toward the gate.

"Who might you men be?" asks General Bishop.

"My name is Ryan, Thomas Ryan. My Uncle Edmond lived here for many years. I came up from Ballyhooly, thinking I'd learn a thing or two about running such a place as this."

The soldier stands erect.

"General, sir… I am on leave from the barracks at Clonmel. Ryan here knows one of these women. We thought to spare you any embarrassment by removing them at once from your gate. Are we violating proper procedures, sir?"

"Procedures? Oh, no. Just get them out of here. Spare me any more local gossip. Ryan, you said? An O'Ryan, you mean? So you're no itinerant cottager? How big is your place down in Bally—"

"Ballyhooly, sir. Father owned fifteen acres of orchards and rented out more. Well, my mother does, now that he's gone. Meantime, I wanted to see a bit of the world myself. My cousin Frank is... was with me, but..."

Tom begins to choke up, then collects himself.

"...he had an accident at the river earlier today. Seems he drowned."

"Just today? Oh, well. I see. Our condolences."

The General pauses briefly.

"Well, then. When you are done, Quinn here will take you up to the house. He shall find a suitable role for you once you're ready. Everything is topsy-turvy these days, so we're short-handed indeed."

The General turns and walks back toward the house. Quinn remains and helps load the bodies into the wagon. The soldier turns and heads back the way he came.

3

———

Bansha

Mr. Quinn and Tom head toward the great house as it looms into view at the end of the path. Tom carries Frank's boots. Toto gives Mr. Quinn a wide berth but keeps Tom in sight. Soon she is in pig heaven, surrounded by garden delicacies scattered across the grounds.

Twin crenellated towers flank the grand entry. As they draw near, Tom sees the familiar fair-haired young woman looking down at him from a second-floor window in the tower on the

right. Another girl, about fifteen, is brushing
Ellen's hair.

Mr. Quinn leads Tom around to a downstairs
kitchen, then takes his leave. A portly woman of
about sixty welcomes Tom.

"Welcome, young man! The General
told me—"

She suddenly recognizes him.

"Begorrah! If it isn't Tom Ryan! Ten years it's
been, if it's been a day!"

"Mrs... Healy?"

"The same! Oh, but it's Quinn now. Poor
Mr. Healy... oh!"

She begins to tear up.

"I'm sorry, ma'am."

"Don't be calling me that now. I'm not the
Queen. Sit, sit, sit! And here—let me take the
muddy boots."

Tom, a little reluctantly, hands them over.

"Oh, but there's something flopping around
in the right one."

She sets down the left boot and turns the
right one over the sink.

"Jesus, Mary, and Joseph! 'Tis a fish!"

Tom says softly, "The Salmon of
Knowledge."

She reaches for the left boot and pulls out a flask of whiskey. She uncorks it and takes a sniff.

"And this? Writer's tears?"

"Knowledge and sadness. Twin spoils of my cousin's travels."

"These are not your own boots, then?"

"My cousin Frank's. He drowned. This very day."

Mrs. Quinn steps back from the sink and blesses herself.

"Dead man's boots?"

Tom presses a reassuring hand on Mrs. Quinn's shoulder.

"A priest blessed them with holy water. Please leave them here. I'll take care of them in the morning. With no body to bury, they're all I have left of him."

"Very well. I'll not cook that fish. But I'll fix you a plate and show you your quarters. You'll be staying here on the west side of the castle."

"The castle, you call it? Tell me—over in the other tower... I saw two young women."

"Young Ellen and poor blind Mary."

"You don't mean my cousin Mary, do you?"

"The same. Lost her sight to a fever."

"But she had no sister, that I recall. The other must be the General's own?"

She takes a seat across from Tom.

"His ward, Ellen. It was all part of the arrangement with your Uncle Edmond. He used the last of his fortune from the sale to set up dowries for the two. He wanted poor Mary to stay in the house."

She leans toward Tom.

"'Tis all she knows. Every nook and cranny. With Ellen to be her eyes."

"But this Ellen, you say—she'd been with my uncle's household?"

Mrs. Quinn leans back in her chair.

"From birth, nearly. An orphan. They never spoke of the circumstances. When guests came to visit, they'd spirit Ellen away. She keeps to herself, mostly. Now, in the old master's time— your uncle's time—well, even now... the Irish landlords, few as they are, always keep close watch on their daughters. The English landlords, it seems, tend to keep a closer watch on their tenants' daughters, if you know what I mean. But since the General arrived, Ellen comes and goes as she pleases."

"This General... Bishop... is he a good man?"

"What can I say?"

She looks first at her outstretched right hand before continuing.

"Half Irish…"

She looks now at her outstretched left hand and continues.

"…half English. A widower. Barely here but a few months of the year. He's the lord of the manor now, so that's that. But oh, I do miss your Uncle Edmond!"

Mrs. Quinn dabs at her eyes with her apron.

"There now, Mrs. Quinn. You were always loyal and true."

She gathers herself, stands, and putters about.

"What shall I fix you in the morning, then? You'd be welcome back here in the kitchen until we settle the arrangements."

Tom gives her a wink.

"Well, I do recall you fix a fine raspberry tart."

EARLY THE NEXT MORNING, Tom sits in the kitchen in the same place, eating his raspberry tart. Mr. Quinn appears in the doorway with a shovel.

"My condolences for your cousin. I suggest you bury his boots in the old O'Ryan family plot. We can arrange for a marker later. Come see me in the office at nine sharp. Mrs. Quinn will show you the way."

After breakfast, Tom makes his way around to the back of the manor house. Toto joins him. He digs a hole by a large ash tree. He sets Frank's boots in the hole, then empties a sack containing the fish in after them. From the same sack, he pulls Frank's whiskey flask, leans against the tree, and takes a swig. He coughs lightly, empties the rest over the grave, then tosses the flask into the hole. He crosses himself and pauses in prayer.

At nine a.m., he stands in the doorway facing Mr. Quinn, who is seated behind a large desk. Mr. Quinn invites Tom in and motions for him to take a seat.

"So, you want to learn how a landlord operates?"

"Landlord? I never thought of my uncle as a landlord, sir. My father said he and his brother prided themselves on never evicting a soul."

Mr. Quinn chuckles.

"Maybe that is why he is gone. How many tenants do you suppose the General has, Tom Ryan?"

"No idea, sir."

"Over 1,400. 1,491, to be precise. No—make that 1,490. One died on Thursday. There once were over 3,000. But whether it's 1,400 or 3,000, I collect the rents from every one of them. It is too much for one man."

"How might I help, sir?"

"We'll come to that. You say your family has fifteen acres down there in Ballyhooly?"

"That is what we own outright. Bought it up acre by acre over the years. But then... we rent another hundred to let out. As my mother explained it to me, my grandfather—her father— took a thirty-one-year lease. That was in the year he returned from the army with Uncle Edmond. They served under General Ponsonby at Waterloo. The lease is up at the end of this year. We have been paying the same rent since 1815."

"Meanwhile, the prices you get have been rising all these years. No doubt, so have the rents your family passes on to your cottagers."

"Oh, no, sir... I mean, I wouldn't know all the

details. But I do know it's been a matter of pride that we never evicted anyone."

Mr. Quinn chuckles again.

"Somehow, I doubt that. Your good mother sounds like a woman of knowledge. Doubtless she does what needs to be done when the time comes. A soldier's wife—and his daughters, even —learn to make decisions when the men are away. What to plant, and when. How to keep good records. How to hire and keep reliable help. When did you say your father passed on?"

"Only last year, before Christmas. But he was a soldier as well and often gone. Our income is mostly from apples. Every last one of them goes off to England. I've never so much as tasted applesauce or a pie from them."

Mr. Quinn smiles kindly.

"Mrs. Quinn can fix that, lad."

"This year we barely got them all picked and sent off, with so many cottagers too sick or hungry to work. The income was enough to cover our own rent this year, but barely. But at least the pigs are fat from the drops."

"And now the harvest is done, your good mother thought she'd send you up here to learn a thing or two—maybe get a little advice?"

"Yes, sir. Quite so."

"She does sound like a woman of knowledge. And it may be a stroke of luck that you'll be getting it from me, not from your poor uncle. No disrespect to your kin, mind—I'm told he was a fine man. But sometimes what it takes is a hard man to get on. Changes are coming to the laws, the General says. Life may get worse before it gets better... for us all."

"So, what might you have in mind for me, sir?"

"My first priority is collecting the rents. But you'll have nothing to do with that. Your conscience can stay clear on that account. I want you to run the manor side. Steward, we'll call it. Farm manager. You'll have room, board, and a fair wage. We'll discuss the details later."

Mr. Quinn extends his hand across the desk, and the two shake on the deal. Tom rises, turns, and exits the office.

IN THE YOUNG LADIES' bedchamber, Ellen opens the curtains to a sunny morning. She is dressed, though her hair still hangs loose. Mary sits at the edge of her twin bed, facing away from Ellen, her eyes downcast.

"What a glorious day! We'll—"

She turns toward Mary.

"Oh dear, is something the matter?"

"Oh, Ellen, I'm so embarrassed. I'm afraid I've soiled myself."

"Let's have a look now... oh..."

Ellen notices a spot on the sheets, then sits beside Mary on the edge of the bed, taking her hand gently.

"Dear Mary, you've had your first visit from the French lady! Nothing shameful at all—not one bit. You are becoming a young woman."

Ellen kisses Mary on the cheek and squeezes her hand.

"You just rest here, and I'll fetch Mrs. Quinn."

"But Ellen, today was our day to go gathering ferns. I was so looking forward to it."

"As was I. But we'll do it again in a few days. Meanwhile, we'll amuse ourselves indoors."

Ellen goes downstairs to find Mrs. Quinn at work.

"Good morning, Mrs. Quinn."

Mrs. Quinn folds a small pile of linens and does not turn to face Ellen.

"A fine good morning to you, Ellen! Are you needing something?"

"Well, it's just... it's Mary... she's, um... she's had her first—"

"—Visit from the French lady. Yes, I know."

Mrs. Quinn chuckles.

"Nothing escapes my eye around here, nor Mr. Quinn's. Each in our own sphere. I was just about to go see to her."

Ellen turns to leave, then stops, pauses, and turns back toward Mrs. Quinn.

"You know, today we were going to take Mary—"

"—Up to the hillside to gather ferns, I know. All the fine young ladies are fern-mad these days. And Mary loves the sounds and smells of the hills."

Mrs. Quinn takes a deep breath and exhales.

"You can still go, dear. Not that you do not come and go as you please, with or without my say-so."

"I won't. Mary is so disappointed she can't. She'd be all the more so if I went without her.

Mmm, I was wondering... about that young man who arrived yesterday."

"Young Tom Ryan. He'll be hiring on as the new... steward, I think is the title. He's Mary's cousin, you know."

"So he's not some pauper who came wandering by."

Mrs. Quinn finally turns to face Ellen, smiling.

"What is your interest, dear girl?"

"Well, perhaps you might ask him to come call. For tea. Perhaps he could share with us what he knows about, you know, conditions in the countryside—or in the towns."

"I'd have thought you were already an expert on that. You know I'd need to speak to the General first. It's one thing to turn a blind eye to your gallivanting around the local hills. Quite another to be receiving a young fellow the General does not know."

"You know the General does not like to be bothered with trifles. Besides, you know him. Mary must know him too, does she not?"

"She'd hardly remember the lad. But I suppose I have some dusting to do there in the drawing room today, round about tea-time."

The older woman smiles discreetly.

"Mrs. Quinn, you're a dear."

Early that afternoon, in the drawing room, Tom and Ellen sit opposite one another, drinking tea. Throughout the conversation, Mrs. Quinn putters about in the background, dusting. She returns to the same spots several times.

Tom expounds; Ellen follows along.

"...and so it all started in on the poor potato plants when, overnight, some foul vapors—"

"A fungus," she says, nodding attentively.

"...yes..." says Tom.

"A water mold, to be precise," she adds.

"It descended in a dense blue fog upon the fields—"

"—During a period of heavy rains."

"...yes... and then, within a few days, we all noticed... we all noticed a heavy, foul—"

"—Stench?" She cocks her head, as a dog might.

"...yes, yes... wait! Am I reporting these events, Ellen, or are you?"

"Sorry. But what I really wondered about

was the people, especially the cottagers who seem to be so badly affected."

"Indeed. We expected to see many destitute people gathered in Mitchelstown, hoping to find food or work. But it seems that as soon as they begin to congregate in any numbers, the constables haul them away to places in the countryside. Out of sight, out of mind. So the streets were surprisingly empty. So dreadful. You would think such a rich nation could provide them with sufficient—"

"—Food?"

"Food... and for the sick, some—"

"—Medicine?"

"Yes, of course," says Tom, "and as the winter approaches—"

"—Clean clothing and shelter? But the General... the General says that if the poor are simply provided handouts, it only encourages dependency. He says this is an Irishman's natural tendency. What do you say, Tom Ryan?"

"Well, if we Irish are such dossers, how do you suppose it is that, when they remove to America, so many of them seem to thrive? Their president, that Jackson fellow who died last year —he was an Irishman, was he not?"

"Or his parents were," says Ellen.

"My cousin Frank would say, 'God sent the blight, but the English created the famine.'"

"And you? What do you say?"

"I think... all men are sinners, not just the English. Misfortunes come, inevitably. Angry mobs only make the problems worse, just as surely as greedy tax collectors and grain merchants do. Faith, hope, and charity are the answer. Without them, all the know-how in the world wouldn't be enough to get on a ship for America—or to stay and plant another crop, knowing the risks."

Ellen pauses and looks down to one side, as if unsure she fully understands.

"An interesting perspective, Tom Ryan."

Off to the side, Mrs. Quinn tips over a bud vase. It smashes to the floor. The conversation ends.

In the young ladies' bedchamber, late that same afternoon, Ellen and Mary sit opposite one another in chairs by the window overlooking the front lawn. Ellen reads aloud from Mary Shelley's Frankenstein:

"Food, however, became scarce, and I often spent the whole day searching in vain for a few acorns to assuage the pangs of hunger. When I found this, I resolved to quit the place that I had hitherto inhabited, to seek for one where the few wants I experienced would be more easily satisfied."

"Oh Ellen, isn't that just like our poor cottagers? So many of them are leaving for America. It saddens me so."

"But Mary, you hardly know them."

"No, I feel I do, even as sheltered as I am. Often on a summer evening, I go to an open window. A breeze will be fresh on my face, and from a distance comes the sound of fiddling, drumming, and pipes."

"Fiddle-dee-dee music, the General calls it. Do you prefer it to my Mozart or Chopin?"

"You know how I love to hear you play, Ellen. But I am not like you. I cannot wander the hills or take a boat out to paddle on the lake—not unless you lead me along. Hearing that simple, bold music makes me feel alive, as much as anything. What a loss it shall be if it goes silent."

Ellen pauses to reflect.

"This book we've been sharing, Frankenstein—are you enjoying it, Mary?"

"Yes, Ellen, I am. Frightful as it is."

"Here's the strangest thing. The woman who wrote it—her mother's name was Wollstonecraft. And this Mary Wollstonecraft was governess to my— to old Mrs. King, when she was a young girl, I mean."

"Mrs. King? I was just thinking of her the other day. She never comes round anymore, not since the General took over. Has something happened to her, I wonder? I used to love her stories—about the faeries and the little people."

"You needn't worry about old Mrs. King. She's fit as a fiddle. I see her from time to time up in the hills. But she does not like the General, for some reason. That is why she keeps her distance. She told me—"

(imitating an old lady's voice)

"'You are such big girls now—young women, that is. You don't need an old busybody like Mrs. King checkin' in on you no more.'"

Mary and Ellen laugh.

"What's that sound?"

"I hear nothing," says Ellen.

"Outside. Animals braying."

Ellen goes to the window, looks around, and fixes her eyes on something.

"Why, two darling little donkeys have wandered onto the lawn!"

In the days that follow, behind the manor and beyond, Tom Ryan throws himself into the everyday farm work around the estate:

He repairs fences around a piggery;

He supervises work on a stone fence around a pasture, where the two little donkeys bray;

He tosses loaves of bread from horseback to laborers as they rest from their work on a drainage ditch.

And so forth. Toto is his constant companion.

One afternoon, Tom shows Ellen the fruits of his labors as she guides Mary along the paths. From a window, the General looks on disapprovingly at the three of them.

On rainy days, in the workshop at the back of the manor, Tom Ryan throws himself into a special project:

First, he planes a length of wood.

Next, he clamps the thin wood into a circlet.

Then, he cuts a piece of leather and stretches it over the frame.

Finally, Tom holds the finished bodhrán in the late-afternoon sunlight and gives it a few resounding beats.

In the young ladies' bedchamber later that afternoon, Mary sits in a chair by the window. Ellen enters the room carrying the bodhrán.

"Mary, dear, please stand and stretch out your hands. I have a little present for you."

Mary giggles.

"Is this where I'm supposed to shut my eyes, if I could see?"

"Yes. Then, it's where you're supposed to say, 'hurry up, the suspense is killing me!'"

"Well...?"

Ellen places the drum into Mary's hands.

"Wha—what is this?"

"You tell me," says Ellen.

Mary rubs her hands all around it. She smiles knowingly and gives it a little thump.

"Why, it's a drum. A bodhrán!"

"Tom Ryan made it for you. He's been working at it in the old shop for days."

Mary smiles and gives it a few more beats.

"Go thank him for me this minute. I do not want an audience while I practice. Not even you!"

Over the next couple of weeks, Mary seeks out private places around the manor grounds to practice playing the bodhrán. In a secluded nook among the garden hedges, an old tenant woman shows her the basic techniques. A few days later, the old woman and her daughter teach her faster rhythms. The three pass bread and the drum between them as they play. On another fine day, two young tenant women dance a traditional step beside her in an arbor.

A week later, Mary plays the bodhrán on the lawn while old Quinn plays the fiddle, Tom plays the tin whistle, and Ellen dances a jig. The General looks out a window at the scene, disapproving.

Each day, at the edge of the grounds, among the trees and hedges, the Hag lurks. She watches the young revelers. She watches the General watching the revelers from his window.

On a rainy Wednesday, the General sits in his library between a large bay window and his massive oak desk. The shelves lining the walls, from floor to ceiling, hold many books on military history and theory: Caesar's The Gallic Wars, Clausewitz's Vom Kriege. The title on one spine reads The Irish Problem. Mr. Quinn sits to the General's right, a few feet away in the corner. Ellen appears in the doorway.

"Good morning, sir. Good morning, Mr. Quinn."

Mr. Quinn nods and looks down.

"Come in, Ellen. Please close the door behind you and take a seat."

Ellen sits with her back to the doorway. A moment of pregnant silence passes as the General regards her sternly. He stands, turns to the window for a moment, then sits again to face her.

"You know, Ellen, that the arrangement I made with your father—your foster father, that is, with Edmond O'Ryan..."

"I always considered Edmond O'Ryan my father, sir, and Mary my sister."

"Of course. And you understand that our arrangement entails certain, erm, fiduciary responsibilities—and more besides. I'm afraid that, with my duties keeping me away so frequently, I have neglected your needs. Last spring, when I was in Africa, we went another season without introducing you properly to society. As the ward of a senior military officer, you could be said to have a certain standing. You speak French well and German passably. You embroider nicely when you set your mind to it. You sing and play beautifully. Not hard to look at, either."

"Sir, I am not sure I understand where this is all leading, but—"

"Yes, yes, you always like to be direct. And so do I. So let me be plain: I won't allow you to become an old maid."

"Sir, I'm eighteen. I hardly think—"

"Nor will I have you gallivanting over hill and dale, acting the flibbertigibbet, or hopping up and down with your poor blind sister like a pair of monkeys to the sound of Irish tom-tom drums."

Mary stands around the corner outside the library, listening. She brings her hands to her mouth in anguish and marches away, brushing a hand along the hallway walls for guidance.

"Spring is a long way off. Meanwhile, Quinn

here will help me draw up a list of promising young men from good families. As if he did not have enough on his plate. We'll invite a few lads to call, once a week or twice a month—with proper supervision."

"You mean to marry me off."

"Dear girl, I am a modern man, not some Hindoo. We do not arrange marriages. My intention is only to expose you to respectable company."

"I have excellent company."

General Bishop cocks an eyebrow and leans over his desk.

"But I must remind you, I do have discretion over your dowry."

"Which I do not consider a honey pot."

Quinn smiles while looking down and away.

"I've thought to make some good use of it," she says, "especially now, for people in need."

The General stiffens.

"As I've said before, Ellen, charity is best left to the Crown and the churches. The strong tenants shall survive. As for the rest, it may be a blessing to see the land cleared of them—convert it from tillage to pasture."

He points toward the ceiling; his face and hands grow more animated.

"Once the rail line comes in, we'll move beef and dairy products to the London market. We'll turn a nice profit."

"Sweetening the honey pot," she says softly, eyes downcast.

"Look, the Liverpool streets are full of Irish vagrants. If the Crown built a Great Wall around England, they'd find a way over, under, or around it. Englishmen are fed up with the costs. 'Irish property should pay for Irish poverty,' they say. By that logic, if this famine grows any worse, it shall bleed us dry!"

Meanwhile, Mary makes her way toward her bedchamber, occasionally feeling along the walls or catching herself as she begins to trip. She slams the door behind her. Inside the room, she cries, screams in frustration, pauses, then begins playing the bodhrán loudly and energetically.

Over the coming weeks, young men come to call.

Ellen receives a young man in the drawing

room. He talks incessantly about nothing, never once looking at her. Ellen yawns. Mrs. Quinn dusts in the background.

Ellen plays the piano for a young man who sips tea and pets a large dog. Mrs. Quinn dusts in the background.

Ellen sits beside a young man on a garden bench. He sniffs a rose. She yawns. Mrs. Quinn shears a hedge in the background.

After every call, Ellen seeks out the same garden bench. There she sits alone, staring into space.

Thus the year passes. None of these would-be suitors calls a second time, despite Ellen's obvious charms. One suffers a bout of hiccups that lasts six months. Another is called away suddenly to Italy; along the way he is abducted by pirates. A third falls in with a band of Travelers and soon begins speaking only the Traveller cant, as if forgetting all knowledge of his native tongue.

MANY WEEKS LATER, on a late afternoon in early 1847, Ellen sits on the same garden bench, exactly where she had sat before, staring into space. Tom Ryan now sits beside her, exactly where the previous young man had sat.

"Daffodils are blooming, yet I don't feel hopeful," she says.

"Mr. Quinn says this year may be even worse than last. He says the new laws will force his hand with the tenants."

"Tom Ryan, have you thought about the question I asked you, up there at the Abbey that day?"

"I have, and I do have a sort of an answer. Came to me in a queer way. Do you want to hear it now?"

Ellen knits her brow.

"I do."

"Well... I think most women—modern women, any woman with a mind of her own..."

Ellen stares straight ahead, expressionless.

"Go on."

"I think any woman wants, or should want, respect. To have a say over her own fate. To be mistress of her household, equal to the man in most ways, more than equal in others. Trusting his judgment in some matters, but never reluctant to have a say."

"And the man? How does a man hold his head high alongside such a woman?"

"I believe... he should accept her counsel willingly, without strain. And she should be free to accept his, or not, without constraint."

"Like 'the quality of mercy.' The quality of love is not strained... or constrained. I do like that."

"Ellen, I wish to ask you something. I feel this moment is as right as any. I know you have other prospects... and I fear what I have to offer is unworthy, but—"

She turns to face him, takes his hands, and smiles—not giddy, but certain.

"—The answer is 'yes.'"

Mrs. Quinn drops a pair of hedge shears in the background.

A FEW DAYS LATER, mid-afternoon, in the manor drawing room, the General sits in an armchair smoking a pipe. Tom sits opposite him. He stirs his tea round and round in the cup.

"I am glad to hear things are going well. Quinn has told me as much."

"Mr. Quinn is a fair man to work for. I'd like to think I've learned much from him."

"Indeed. Now, what was it you've come to ask me, Ryan? I do have an inkling, so you may as well get to the point."

"Yes, sir. It's about your ward, Ellen. I have asked for her hand. We wish to marry, with your blessing."

"I see."

The General draws on his pipe.

"You know, Ryan... if Ellen were my own daughter, it would be out of the question. As the daughter of a senior military officer, she would be far above your station."

"'Would be,' Sir? In my eyes, she is indeed above my station. But I would do anything to make myself worthy."

"Anything, Ryan? If you are sincere, then I have a proposal."

"Sir?"

"I should like you to serve under my command in Africa for, shall we say, a year... before revisiting the matter. If you perform well, I may even be able to work around normal procedures. To, shall we say, advance you. Make you a more suitable match for the girl."

"I see."

Tom draws a breath. There is a barely audible commotion in the hallway.

"Not that I care a whit about society gossip. I am a modern man. But I do take my duty to the girl seriously, and my obligations to your uncle. He did love the girl as his own daughter, I believe. He served the Crown honorably. Gave his right arm at Waterloo. And all of that."

Mrs. Quinn steps into the doorway. She enters the room gingerly, a few paces in.

"Sir, I know you wished not to be interrupted. But the old woman... the old woman..."

The Hag pushes her way into the room.

"The old woman insisted she be received," croaks the Hag. "And the old woman has excellent hearing. The old woman, you see, has an interest in this matter."

"What the devil—?"

The General stands.

"You! What 'interest' is this of yours? Speak!"

"You see, dear General, this young man... Tom Ryan, here... is bound to me."

"What the—"

He looks at Tom.

"Ryan, what business have you with this busybody?"

"Sir, I made a promise to the good woman."

The General sneers.

"'Good woman?' Ryan, are you engaged to another? If so, you'll be out on your ear!"

"No, sir, nothing like that. She came to my aid once. I promised to grant her one request in return."

"Quite so," says the Hag. "Let me get to the point. My request is this: Tom Ryan shall not leave Ireland. He shall not take up arms against his fellow man."

"Wait," says Tom. "That is two requests. I agreed only to honor one."

The Hag looks momentarily confused.

"Oh, right... well then... well..."

She now looks annoyed.

"Who are you, bucko, the grammar police? I shall rephrase it. You shall never leave Ireland to serve in the Crown's stupid bloody foreign wars. There. Fixed."

Tom looks a little sheepish.

"I see. Truly, sir, I am bound to honor this woman's request... even if it means the General withdraws his blessing."

The General speaks without irony.

"Young Ryan, I see you are a man of integrity. Not everyone is cut out to be a soldier."

The General retakes his seat and his pipe. Meanwhile, Ellen has been listening from around the corner of the drawing-room doorway. She steps well into the room. Toto the pig follows her in and stops at her side.

"I must speak. Please, no one interrupt. Tom Ryan is an honorable man. Yes, like any woman, I long to be mistress of my own home. What I want all the more is a man of honor who is true to his word. I will take his hand in marriage, with or without anyone else's blessing."

At that, Toto bites the hem of the Hag's dirty cloak and drags it to the floor, along with her long gray-haired wig.

The General looks the Hag up and down, then suddenly recognizes her.

"Gad! Lady Edith!"

"The very same. Edith King Fitzgerald of Mitchelstown Castle. Once my home, now fallen, as I am, to wrack and ruin. And this Ellen is my own dear orphaned grandchild. Eighteen years ago, her mother died bringing her into this world. Ever since, I have kept my eye on the child. With all my remaining fortune, influence, and powers, it is I who shall bless this marriage!"

The General stands.

"Influence? Fortune? Powers? You old busybody! Wandering the glen, up and down the mountain, poking your nose into everyone's affairs? Trafficking in spells, people say. Caused the potato blight, even, people say! This, this... hobbledehoy... has no business whatever marrying the ward of a British General!"

Lady Edith snickers. She stands erect now, dignified in bearing.

"Fine words of praise you had a moment ago for young Ryan here, when it suited your purpose. Do you suppose you'd be having the dear girl for yourself, despite the difference of age and station? As for the local gossip, have you any idea who the local folk said it was who abandoned her mother eighteen years ago? A certain young captain, no?"

General Bishop turns red in the face.

"Hush, woman!"

Lady Edith glares at the General and lifts her staff high, as if to strike it down hard against the floor.

Ellen rushes forward to grasp Lady Edith's right arm.

"Mamó, no! Not that!"

Lady Edith, looking sheepish, sets her staff down gently.

"Oh, I suppose you're right, dear girl. My work is near done. Time to retire my blue bottle and strive to do the Lord's work, in the Lord's way. Abide by the law, abide by the Church..."

Ellen addresses her affectionately.

"That's right. Time to behave yourself, as a little old lady should."

Outside the window, the raven caws twice. Tom, Ellen, and Lady Edith proceed toward the manor's front door. Mary joins them. The doors swing open, and they walk through, their backs silhouetted against the bright late-afternoon sunlight. The donkeys bray.

The four walk down the manor path to the gate, where a wee man with the look of a leprechaun sits in the back of a large wagon. His legs dangle over the edge as he casually eats an apple. Behind him are a large famine pot and sacks of grain. Up front, Paddy holds the reins.

Tom, Ellen, and Mary approach the wagon. Lady Edith stands aside by the gate.

"Hop in," says the leprechaun.

EPILOGUE

That evening in 1933, in the large bedroom of a house in Meriden, Connecticut, a little red-haired girl of about four sits on Molly's lap. A boy of about eight plays with toy airplanes on the floor. The three of them sit within the circle of a large, worn, braided rug. A fire burns in the background. Molly continues the story, reciting it by heart as she learned it from her mother, here and there adding her own embellishments.

"In the years after the famine had taken its terrible toll, Ellen and Tom raised a family. Mary O'Ryan married Finn Murphy's son, Jimmy. They dwelt on the last remainder of Edmond

O'Ryan's land. With the money from Frank's saddle, Jimmy bought some calves. They started a dairy at Rossadrehid."

"Was that far away from... from... Bally-booly?" asks the girl, Una.

"Ballyhooly. No, not too far."

Molly continues the story.

"Local folk said Jimmy was so ugly, blind Mary and the cows were the only girls who'd have him. But they prospered by their own labors. Lady Edith schooled them all well in the ways of the Other People, until her time came."

"One of the children, Nana Lizzie, carried this story off to Connecticut. She left it in her steamer trunk from Ireland, on a piece of wrinkled paper tucked into an old pair of horsehide shoes—lest we ever forget our people's hardships and joys."

"Wait!" says the boy, Tim. "No more scary parts? C'mon!"

"Well, all right then—just for boys... but it's not really part of the story!

"In the graveyard at Glanworth Abbey, by the light of a full moon, three banshees rise from the graves into the sky. The Galtee Mountains are silhouetted against the moonlit night. The banshees fly over the mountains toward the O'Ryan manor.

"The manor is now overgrown with vines. From a second-story window, a shutter hangs askew. The sound of wind howls and taps on the windows... tap! tap! TAP!

"As for the aging General, from that year forward the grand house would never know the sound of laughter again. Instead, it was haunted by the dead widows of soldiers who had perished in the Afghan wars or in Zululand under his command. They are said to dwell amid the ruins of Glanworth Abbey, whence they fly on November Eve over the Galtee Mountains toward the once-grand O'Ryan home, known to the common folk today as the Banshee Castle. There they rap, rap, rap at the windows with assegai spears and wail pitifully until dawn."

"The Banshee Castle? Your own little twist on the Bansha Castle? Or was it a child's mistake made long ago?" Asks Quill with a grin. "Ah, well, never let the truth get in the way of a good story!" He winks.

"General Bishop tosses and turns in his bed.

"Meanwhile, within the walls, a fair lenanshee spirit torments the lonely master's dreams, night after night and year after year, until he wastes away to skin and bones."

On the rug, Tim makes airplane engine and machine-gun sounds. Molly scowls, then smiles, and ushers the children into their twin beds. She kisses them goodnight, turns out the light, and goes downstairs to the parlor.

QUILL, the man from the line that morning, sits next to her brother Tom in front of a crackling fire. Their faces glow in the firelight. The little man holds the transcribed tale in his lap.

"A queer tale we have here. 'Boy meets girl' in the middle of the dreadful famine? Well, it must have happened. Some of us wouldn't be here if it hadn't. As for the rest, it's up to you to sort out what's malarkey and what ain't. Those last bits I overheard you weaving in, about the General? Malarkey. I know of him. By all accounts, he was a decent enough man. He lived out his days in contentment."

Molly chuckles. "A little poetic license, is all, Quill."

"The Banshee Castle? Your own little twist on the Bansha Castle? Or was it a child's mistake made long ago?" asks Quill with a grin. "Ah, well—never let the truth get in the way of a good story!" He winks.

"What about the soldier at the manor house gate?" Tom asks.

"That may well have been Patrick Sheehan. If you don't know his story—and this is no malarkey—he was blinded in the Crimean War. No loving family about him, as your Blind Mary had. His pension back in Ireland, six pence a day, lasted nine months. So he wandered the streets of Dublin as a mendicant until a magistrate jailed him for begging. Arrested in 1857 on Grafton Street. There is a song about him. Shall I sing it for you, Molly and Tom? Quietly, so as not to wake the children? I make no promises for my voice."

"Oh!" says Molly. "Please do!"

"Imagine a busy modern sidewalk, a graying busker singing it, not I:

'... So Irish youths, dear countrymen, take heed in what I say

For if you join the English ranks, you'll surely rue the day

And whenever you're tempted, a-soldiering
to go

Remember poor blind Sheehan from the
Glen of Aherlow…'"

AN OCEAN AWAY, early in the morning of the
present day, at a crossroads along the road from
Mitchelstown to Ballyhooly, a pickup truck
lumbers south. Two young men—fit hikers on
foot, heading north—pause at the far side of the
intersection.

A sign points right, west toward Castletown
Roche, and straight ahead, south, toward
Ballyhooly.

The truck turns west onto the road toward
Castletown Roche.

The two hikers doff their caps. Seated in the
back of the truck, a wee man with the look of a
leprechaun raises his right hand and waves. One
of the hikers starts after him.

"I've seen the wee fellow! At a pub in Cork
City. A fine storyteller!"

The older one holds him back.

"We've our own stories now. Our own craic

to find, straight ahead and over the hill. Come along!"

A cloud of dust rises behind the truck, obscuring the hikers from view.

120

THE END

ABOUT THE AUTHOR

T.A. Keenan graduated from the University of Chicago and Georgetown University. He writes from a small farm near the Appalachian Trail in central Maryland. *Tom Ryan's Shoes*, originally written as a screenplay, is his first novel.

https://takeenan.com/

https://www.facebook.com/takeenan.fiction/